Praise for

MY INDEX OF SLIGHTLY HORRIFYING KNOWLEDGE

"Guest takes the reader on a path like few contemporary poets offer."
—*Chicago Sun-Times*

"Irreversible, permanent physical damage would seem less a potential source of art than an obstacle to it: it will not lend itself to the work of imagination; it will not, in a different light, seem a different thing; it is more powerful as a fact than anything that could be said about it. Paul Guest does not sentimentalize disaster; it remains irreversible, immense—and yet it emerges that there are things to be said, about it and through it, I would not have imagined. An urgent and moving book." —Louise Glück

"Paralyzed in a bicycle accident at age twelve, Guest as an adult has turned his serious anger, his irrepressible energies, and his sex drive into an instantly recognizable and passionate style. . . . The poems race, churn, and tumble over themselves with a welcome, often R-rated, power of invention. Guest might be Percy Bysshe Shelley crossed with Nick Flynn, or Neruda fused with Dean Young, at once perpetually dissatisfied and breathless with anticipation. . . . Guest's fast-paced, sometimes even offensive third volume could be a poetry hit."
—*Publishers Weekly* (starred review)

"The invalid's rage . . . and the ridiculousness of it all inform Paul Guest's wonderful poems, flung one after another in the teeth of 'daily' life, each an act of defiance that affirms the terrible power of that life. One thinks of Elizabeth Bishop's lines 'the fiery event / of every day in endless / endless assent.'"
—John Ashbery, author of *Notes from the Air*
and *Where Shall I Wander*

"A beautiful, breathless torrent of language that is dark or insightful or funny or any combination thereof, but always on the mark, always riveting. . . . *My Index of Slightly Horrifying Knowledge* is a terrific book. "
—Mark Strand

"It's a horrible spiritual truth that the greatest suffering yields the greatest wisdom, and in Paul Guest's affliction (he's paralyzed) he knows the radical powerlessness of the human unit that all of us are in the process of learning. And he knows about death. Yet there's tremendous sexual force in many of these poems and also, always, blessedly unstoppable humor. Guest is a spirit to be reckoned with. Here's a body of new work to cheer about."
—Mary Karr

"A seemingly bottomless gas tank of generosity fuels these high-octane poems—generosity of spirit, language, charm, empathy, wisdom, and ironic goodwill in the face of even the most callous misfortunes. Like the American culture he documents, Paul Guest's poetry is both funny and serious, surreal and hyper-real, lyrically self-incriminating and apocalyptically compassionate. *My Index of Slightly Horrifying Knowledge* is a terrific book by a poet we should all read."
—Campbell McGrath, author of *Seven Notebooks*

ALSO BY PAUL GUEST

Exit Interview

Notes for My Body Double

The Resurrection of the Body and the Ruin of the World

One More Theory About Happiness

c.1

MY INDEX OF SLIGHTLY HORRIFYING KNOWLEDGE

PAUL GUEST

An Imprint of HarperCollinsPublishers

HarperCollins books may be purchased for educational, business, or sales promotional use. For information, please write: Special Markets Department, Harper-Collins Publishers, 10 East 53rd Street, New York, NY 10022.

An extension of this copyright page appears on page 82.

A hardcover edition of this book was published in 2008 by Ecco, an imprint of HarperCollins Publishers.

FIRST ECCO PAPERBACK EDITION PUBLISHED 2010.

Designed by Ralph Fowler

Library of Congress Cataloging-in-Publication Data is available upon request.

ISBN: 978-0-06-168519-4

10   11   12   13   14   OV/RRD   10   9   8   7   6   5   4   3   2   1

For Eliot Khalil Wilson

CONTENTS

User's Guide to Physical Debilitation   1

My Life Among   3

Airport Letter 1   5

Rented Dark   6

Poem Written to Replace Another   8

Poem Written outside Wintry Mix   10

Audio Commentary Track 1   12

Loyalty Oath   14

A Brief History of History   16

My Past   17

Early in a New Year   18

My Crush   19

The Lives of the Optimists   20

One More Theory about Happiness   21

Eulogy   22

Valentine   23

To-Do List   24

Towards a Theory of Proximity   25

Elegiac Forecast   27

Remember How Sad That Was When   28

Things We Agreed Not to Shout   29

Audio Commentary Track 2   30

My Index of Slightly Horrifying Knowledge   32

Oblivion: Letter Home 1   38

Oblivion: Letter Home 2   40

Oblivion: Letter Home 3   42

Poison   44

Regarding Your Applications for Many Imaginary Positions   45

Job   46

My Nightmare   48

Bad Mood   49

Accent   51

My Arms   52

Preemptive Elegy   53

Airport Letter 2   55

Travel   56

Semi-Apocalyptic R.S.V.P. with Contingencies   58

Seduction with Monomyth   61

Bordering on the Tragic   63

Elegy for the Plesiosaur on the Advent of Its Predicted Return   64

Praise   66

At Night, in November, Trying Not to Think of Asphodel   68

Beginning in the Lost and Unclaimed Baggage Center in
Scottsboro, Alabama   70

Austria   72

Elegy for the Lumbering Monster   74

A Long Time I've Wanted to Say Something   76

My Luck   78

My Mock-Scale Dream   80

Acknowledgments   81

MY
INDEX
OF
SLIGHTLY
HORRIFYING
KNOWLEDGE

USER'S GUIDE TO
PHYSICAL DEBILITATION

Should the painful condition of irreversible paralysis
last longer than forever or at least until
your death by bowling ball or illegal lawn dart
or the culture of death, which really has it out
for whoever has seen better days
but still enjoys bruising marathons of bird watching,
you, or your beleaguered caregiver
stirring dark witch's brews of resentment
inside what had been her happy life,
should turn to page seven where you can learn,
assuming higher cognitive functions
were not pureed by your selfish misfortune,
how to leave the house for the first time in two years.
An important first step,
with apologies for the thoughtlessly thoughtless metaphor.
When not an outright impossibility
or form of neurological science fiction,
sexual congress will either be with
tourists in the kingdom of your tragedy,
performing an act of sadistic charity;
with the curious, for whom you will be beguilingly blank canvas;
or with someone blindly feeling their way
through an extended power outage
caused by summer storms you once thought romantic.
Page twelve instructs you how best
to be inspiring to Magnus next door
as he throws old Volkswagens into orbit
above Alberta. And to Betty
in her dark charm confiding a misery,
whatever it is, that to her seems equivalent to yours.
The curl of her hair that her finger knows
better and beyond what you will,
even in the hypothesis of heaven
when you sleep. This guide is intended
to prepare you for falling down

and declaring détente with gravity,
else you reach the inevitable end
of scaring small children by your presence alone.
Someone once said of crushing
helplessness: it is a good idea to avoid that.
We agree with that wisdom
but gleaming motorcycles are hard
to turn down or safely stop
at speeds which melt aluminum. Of special note
are sections regarding faith
healing, self-loathing, abstract hobbies
like theoretical spelunking and extreme atrophy,
and what to say to loved ones
who won't stop shrieking
at Christmas dinner. New to this edition
is an index of important terms
such as catheter, pain, blackout,
pathological deltoid obsession, escort service,
magnetic resonance imaging,
loss of friends due to superstitious fear,
and, of course, amputation
above the knee due to pernicious gangrene.
It is our hope that this guide
will be a valuable resource
during this long stretch of boredom and dread
and that it may be of some help,
however small, to cope with your new life
and the gradual, bittersweet loss
of every God damned thing you ever loved.

MY LIFE AMONG

I'm beginning to dream again of my life among
the ornamental, the vaguely functional,
the doorstops and paperweights, my tenure
in the legion of lawn gnomes, my brotherhood
with novelty decanters, my solidarity
with the generally useless, the inscrutably devised,
the deformed idea, the Elvis clock,
the flea market phantasm, the broken
stapler clicking toothlessly, the pen caddy unpenned,
I'm driving towards nowhere,
I'm listening to the station
broadcasting the weather,
I'm forgetting the weather,
I'm shutting my vinyl coat in the car door,
I'm leaving it there in the door
like a strange maroon pelt,
I'm dreaming of all the use I could have been
but was not, the clock repairman
lost in the Swiss coils of time,
eyes ruined by the hours
and the hours, the antiquated milkman
leaving frost-rimed bottles
on the doorstep of a 1950's educational film,
that burred boy at the door
terrified by the split atom,
by Sputnik, by his mother's zombie absolution,
that was not me, no, not so
specific as that, not this morning
which is not the same
morning in my dream, strange
to think now there are two
of them, one in which my name is Paul Guest
and one in which I can't read
the tag pressed to my chest
or the name on my birth
certificate, nothing in this morning
speaks any language

I know, maybe I've fallen into the mind's endless
Russia, maybe this dream
has piled against my mind
like snow and the cold radiates everywhere,
through the windows and the door
it comes like a battering
ram, announcing itself with splinters,
but no dream ever lasts,
not even the terrifying ones,
the ones from which all floors have fled
and everything is gravity
and velocity and at the dream's end is death.

AIRPORT LETTER 1

In Greensboro the trees spasm with ache or what
I'll say is ache. Better to pretend winter
never came with its hands full of Canada.
Better to watch them sway this always
farewell. Better to do many things than this.
One more book I won't finish
and artesian water and muffins
like wagon wheels want my wallet
to open like a flower. Nobody laughs
when I say Kim Jong Il is my copilot,
nobody but me, and in this
there is a lonesome perfection
found high above one's life.
I am advised the cushion beneath me will float
should we find ourselves in water
and I'm informed of the invention
of the seat belt. All its mysteries
tumble out into this tube of air
we'll call our own and in it
the smell of us goes forth—
it isn't bad, not when
you've burned by mistake
a bag of dog hair,
as I did one summer that now feels
like amnesia. But this odor is communal,
countless cells pushing
salt from the skin like a greeting.
A congress of nerves.
So I think of you beside me,
your body knotted with dreams.
How the sky can seem an intrusion,
all this blue like an ocean, an ur-sea.
Something in which to vanish. To sink like stones.

RENTED DARK

Even priapic bouts of sexual insanity
were no match against that winter
which dropped snow like cement
for cement's sake. I came to think
of the weather as one of the leering
prison guards in a *Women in Chains* flick,
cast for his ability to produce
terrifyingly profuse body hair
and an admirably effortless mien of depravity.
Breakfast became bananas
and anthropomorphizing the storms
or thoughtfully vetoing
each other's baroquely murderous impulses
or speaking to each other
in the flat affect of hostages
denouncing the moral and ethical whatever
of wherever. I dreamed
of understanding the sky
or touching your skin somewhere
beyond the bit of darkness we rented
on Olympic Street
without fearing we'd lose a thumb or toe
or dawdle into hypothermia
like lost children.
But that was when I dreamed
or slept at all. At night by light of the busted TV,
it was easy to see how
your face fell into sleep
and the rest of you followed
while each infomercial taught me
how to be wowed
by borrowed yachts
and stock photographs of Italian roadsters
and grimly orgasmic head cases
who waved cancelled checks like stays of execution
while swilling soda water
with Pentecostal fury.

There were *secret methods*
and *proven techniques*
and when I closed my eyes
it sounded like birth control from an alternate dimension.
Supplies were low.
I had to order now
but I never did,
letting the night run out
like the special offer each one was.
While we made love
in a frozen world, operators stood by.

POEM WRITTEN TO
REPLACE ANOTHER

There was a long sentence I wanted to say
in the dream, about life in America,
about the literature of apocalypse
or living in caves, or living within earshot
of trains. Which is to say I don't
recall a thing that I dreamed last night,
the color of anything, the tenebrous custard of clouds,
the water that fell in shapes
from the elm trees. Really, what I'm thinking
tonight is there is nothing
in all the flat world which would satisfy me.
Not food and not love and no
Epicurean kink involving both
and in this I am trying to feel only
a little sad. Slightly broken.
Returnable, still, even to the ones I loved,
their darling, imperious airs,
their hair in careless garlands
announcing one more morning or one last.
They went about in the immediacy
of dreams. They said, or did not
say, I am the tacit light of the stars.
A long time it took me
to make sense of that
and longer still their absences,
which felt like nothing
of the sort, though through them I could hear
trains warning the miles
of their torturous approach.
It seems beautiful,
to think now of that sound
which is all immensity and inevitability
and other abstractions
which only call to mind
everything that is too easy to be forgotten:

that winter is not endless
or without charm,
at least for those who find it charming,
and I am not one,
hovering beside the thermostat
with a safecracker's impenetrable intent.
Love, it is cold out there,
is not what I mean
with every adjustment of the worn dial,
but I might say it,
were you to ask,
stranger who doesn't know me at all.

POEM WRITTEN OUTSIDE
WINTRY MIX

Meaning, I am separate. The speakers lurch
music I can't love, I can't tell you
I love you. The window is obvious
and cold and the climate's breath
fogs it up, the world outside hindered.
I think that is the word I want
but it may be that I come
to you in the inconvenient darkness
saying I have not meant
myself for a very long time. It may be
that I stub my life black
and nearly weep, limping
away. It will be funny one day,
wait and see. This wound
and the next made nothing
at all by time's mad gush of speed.
We'll laugh, though now all
there is is the slush filling
the gutter up with inconstant diamonds.
I owed you something,
once, and you were good
enough to bear me
forgetting you. Your hands
older than you were,
even in the night, graspsome, close.
Outside, the world is
stupid with whiteness
and cloud wet. I can't think
of numbers meant
to identify me or cities by which I'm ruled.
I can't think of this
effect my breath makes
of the air but
by it I can tell

you that I am not dead,
or that I've stumbled into the cold,
thinking of this
dream.

As you can already see, everything is fucked.
I really can't remember why
but we hadn't slept in three days,
downing rubbing alcohol by the bottle
and falling into stuporous public sex
at skating rinks and professional wrestling matches.
And there were the strange dares:
someone had heard lethally ascetic Canadian monks
were able to cause their intestines
to erupt in horrifying geysers from their abdomens
and all of us wanted to be the first
to figure out the trick of it.
So maybe in context you'll understand
why most of the movie is missing sound
as we come to know this painfully shy woman.
Why Samantha weeps during sex
or is emotionally unavailable
to the people who need her most—
the dullards in the inexact change lane.
That we all forgot to rig the microphones
really does challenge the audience
to stay with the story by reading lips.
Or by accurately guessing her thoughts
as she naps on the sofa under general anesthesia.
And her feelings for this man
unlike any she's known before
with his toothless optimism and total amnesia.
If you're able to overlook how close
we all were to massive organ failure,
you'll see some magic. Like this shot
of a tear streaking down her cheek
and through the precipitous ravine of her cleavage.
They were real, I should add, the tears.
The producer would call from Bogotá
where he had arranged
for her children to be tutored in cages.
The shoot was hard on everyone

12

and the parasites didn't help
so I tried to keep the atmosphere light.
Which was hard to do
when everyone suffered from 106 degree fevers
and clinically undiagnosed paranoia.
But we pushed through
because we cared about the story
and eventually bothered to look at the dailies.
The only scene with sound was the last.
Which seemed almost poetic.
Above the landfill and their naked bodies,
above their clothes left in hurried heaps,
a choir of gulls are sadly cawing.
To me each convulsive sob sounds like joy.

LOYALTY OATH

Solemnly do I swear and affirm and affix
many foil seals with arcane symbols
to the lividly carcinogenic spirit
of Senator Joseph Raymond McCarthy
of Wisconsin, a state I like
for letting Matt live there in happiness
with his wife, for being the only place of birth
Karri is likely to have. And further
do I tiresomely swear with my face
made up in moral gravity that in most ways
I am fucking awesome
and not a subversive person interested in
or committed to the overthrow of governments
by violence, disobedience or denial
of gym membership. I swear
upon many stacks of leather bound Bibles
the Gideons leave in hotel rooms
where I often went with lovers
to roll around for entire weekends
in sheets we fouled with ourselves and Chinese takeout.
I swear on your mother's grave
and the fresh one beside her
where your father sleeps beneath new sod.
On my children screaming inside me
to hurry up and create them
with a foolish but lovely woman.
On her body's every curve
by which I know how not to grow lost
when all there is to see by
is the moon tumbling from the sky
and the alarm clock's red math.
I swear this and avow that
and sometime I promise
to promise to never violate
the Geneva Convention in all its charming quaintness.
I depose and declare
and many other verbs

which sound wondrously stern.
I lay down with my heart
and my hand above it
and both are filled with blood
and every breath swears its false oath so help me God.

If alchemists ever surrendered to common sense,
I'm not sure my mailbox noticed,
everyday coughing up a wealth
of free credit, a siren's song of silk
in the free bras promised me
(or current resident) by each coupon
in touching good faith. The infinite
has never beckoned so well
I want to follow after it
into further confusion. The Chinese
in searching for life eternal
found instead galvanic black powder.
For whole years potions were heated
over low fires set in clay earth,
tended to at the cost of their lives.
Sent to the green eastern seas
with five hundred boys
and five hundred girls,
Xu Fu never returned. Who can blame him?
This was never my dream,
to live beyond the code coiled in my cells,
to live longer than the mountain
above me or the river
at my side like a woman. Like you in moonlight.
Except we never sleep
with windows up or the shades undrawn
so it's a lie to say I've seen you
glowing with irradiated time.
Better to say I've seen you
barely at all. Better to say
the lost moon will never guide us.
Better to cover you
beside the eastern sea
with lapidary jade
fat emperors ate hoping not to die.

16

MY PAST

I was young and needed the porn but not
the money or the long seasons
of shame or whatever was the burning
sensation I felt in my head
trying to sleep or pretend
I was dead as kids pelted me
with gravel or home-brewed napalm
that I could not deny,
even in the invidious gravity of such pain,
was impressive. Skin
grew back like the grass
in which I slept with all my green
dreams, all my terror
and my pockets full
of stolen salt and crushed acorns,
which are poisonous
to humans. There are things
I know of so little worth
I resent them their place
in this pot of meat my head is.
Saying it needs a hat. Or a scented pillow
stuffed with the extravagance
of goose flight. Once I wanted wings.
And once a getaway car,
not to mention
the jet pack cobbled from a leaf blower
or the millions needed
for *bon voyage*
in my own manned luxury submersible
or a zeppelin parked
above our heads and
wavering in the air like escape.

EARLY IN A NEW YEAR

Maybe scientists have found Mozart's skull
and it's possible one man has brought
back from extinction the miniature zebra
called the quagga, but in both cases
genetic tests are not conclusive. List for me,
would you, what this world knows
about the next. And the ones in a chain
beyond these. Draw out the diagram
that will prove the rate of decay
in that star, that cobalt flicker
we see each night in bed, and
in the calcium lode that is my femur, my thigh
where your hands, your mouth
have been—show me how it's true
I'm receding from you like a star
and I won't sleep at all. Dissolve
the endless parade of dumb
that is this story I keep professing
each morning. It isn't me that dreams of me
orbiting the moon like a moth,
I swear. Somewhere within there is
an impudent cell that recalls
some other life, some other apple green world.
When I'm quiet and still,
when I stop speaking out
to the motion of the water ringing the drain,
I listen like a child to the darkness
where monsters sing.

MY CRUSH

I never saw more of your unsunned skin than
the bus driver or the chainsaw salesman
or that waitress in that barely viable town,
unless they saw more than me
by accident or arrangement
or some other calculus of random passion
I don't even want to consider
and yet here I've invited
all of us into the present tense
as though it were a garden party
exploding with gladiolas
and polite sipping and pained
concern for the lacerated kidneys
of someone distant, half-known but in that light
assigned a measure of imminence
which seems proper
to everyone in accord
before that pain is exhausted
as pain always is
and everyone begins to shimmer
in their own pains,
the knees in name only,
spines full of wire, fused bone and pain management,
vein stripped
from the arm
like a black weed,
and wherever I am in all of this
or wherever all of this is within me,
through the gate into dusk you've gone like the day.

THE LIVES OF THE OPTIMISTS

So the jonquils are fooled into flaming up
though it's January. The bricks soak
in heat like ruddy sponges.
Walking home, I hide
within whatever's radiant.
A bird whose name I've never bothered
to learn sings its farewell
to winter. It's January. Tomorrow
we'll grieve. Or the next
day, but not this thawed instant,
not in this false blush
of lilac. In my bones, the old scores
with the earth are laid to rest
and each dyspeptic grudge
blossoms into frantic, sweet, careening
love. In your bones,
the tidal hymns of blood.
This heedless smile once was yours.
So too my hands,
themselves fooled
by the tilt of the earth, the white face of a star.

ONE MORE THEORY
ABOUT HAPPINESS

That it comes to you like an accident
with a powder-actuated nail gun,
that it's wisdom of the sort
you hear in line with your cargo
of toothpaste, detergent, condoms,
salt, whatever has appeared
on the vacant horizon of the day
like ink smudge or birds on the wing
for Mexico. That it multiplies
with the mythic, sexual frenzy of the rabbit,
which you regard, now,
like Fellini played backwards
at half speed. That whole libraries
to it are devoted like pious
women in a foreign country,
perhaps Spain, their white hair ignored.
That you will reap it
according to what you sow.
That you will speak of it
the way you remember an unread book.
That you'll find it.
That in eternity your keys find you.
That desire is the cause
of all human suffering
according to Buddha,
according to the man whose arms dead-end
at the bulbs of his elbows
kicking a dog
from the sidewalk with savage joy.
That the dog in this
matter has no say,
except to articulate miniature outrage.
That it is better to have no arms than four legs.

EULOGY

So that this will seem like words between
old friends, I'll say it was painless.
And quick. I'll say it was mercy
and behind my face where I put
things like The Truth and dreams about
supernovae, I'll try to mean it.
But it was his time, we should all admit.
Shouldn't we, who loved him
the way we love traffic
and cell phones during spectacular sex
and the degradations of puberty,
shouldn't we all feel
as though light were swelling within us,
inflaming us? Tell me where
you were when you heard
but tell me later, much later,
the kind of later mathematicians get excited about.
By then memory will have torn
away from my body like a scab
I'll no longer have to pick at
and I'll listen to you like a stethoscope.
It will be good for my heart.
It will be good for your heart.
In the air of that deferred spring
we'll be healthy, speaking
of an ancient wound neither of us
really remember, except
that by starlight we promised
to honor this question mark
in the periodic sentence of our lives.
Whatever you say, remember
that we cried. The dead love that we weep.

That we stain ourselves with
salt, that we become for a moment
indistinguishable from the sea.
That our shining faces rock with grief.

VALENTINE

Tell me to sleep, to be still, to root.
All atoms, star litter, my body.

I practice breath like an arcane trick.
To the afterthought night

makes of your hair
I'm saying *nuzzle*,

pneumatic with fear I said *nozzle*.
Or the rain I want

to be snow
and the snow I wish were ashes,

ashes. Tell me not
to burn, to burrow, to seek dark soil.

Tell me not.
Beside you, my weight in blood

and my lungs dreaming
of the silent ocean

floor. This is my shell, beloved, and these,
my claws. When

you speak to me
like the vivisected moon,

you are mine.

TO-DO LIST

A lot you should do: hurl invective at dawn.
Stop at dusk. Stop all attempts
at rhetorically complex valentines
as timed to the sun or any star
available for general reference. Mow the lawn
or at least remove the rust
clotted bear traps from the thicket
all the lawn has slowly become
in a kind of melancholy art installation
you want to watch forever. Definitively determine
the distance between thinking
and doing. Once and for all. For it is vast.
And submit the results
to many peer-reviewed journals
hoping to give so much thinking and doing
to oblivion. For it too is vast.
And full of fondness for however much
you're content to ignore
its tab for the ruin it keeps running up
everywhere you care to look. And those places
you don't. Don't think
there isn't a spot for you
in all this abstraction; you'll fit right in
and never look back at that
world again. How her skin
and your skin, how both were one world
while her red hair burned
you through the chest, through to the bone
and to the well of blood
where she held you
up and all you carried, all that you had in you
like an ore, you gave. Give

again.

TOWARDS A THEORY
OF PROXIMITY

I'm not even sure what that might mean,
not in a world of numbered meaning,
in which I'm close to sloped elm shade,
it falls against my door weighing
nothing at all but I love it just the same,
and I am near train tracks where
I stop sometimes to watch the loudness
of the cars bearing glittery coal
away to a mouthy, pitched fire,
and that I'm not near that
blossom of flame, burning the recovered
dead, it kills me some nights
because I have thought,
leaning my weight against the door,
picking at the peeling strip
meant to stop seeping cold from slipping in,
picking at it like a wound,
with this stick I hold in
my mouth, all because I have thought
of a woman's hand, water
she bore in glass back to the bed
we'd share like it was air
or candy, a surfeit of rain
beneath a brick arch where once
we kissed a long time,
and that water she gave me first to drink,
and how cold it was
nothing could prepare me for,
as though the faucet was
those midwestern mornings made of ice,
and everything seemed near,
my body to hers, hers to mine,
it seems false now, the attempt
to parse our flesh

or say that her skin
meant anything more
than mine to me now means, tonight,
but it doesn't stop me
from saying a thing,
saying this, every word a wish, a blank invitation.

ELEGIAC FORECAST

May God bless and keep the last man
struggling with galoshes, which means
French shoes in Old French and who knew
the French had ever been fond
of their feet sheathed in onomatopoeic
footwear or that their tongues
had in the dead past divagated and dithered
whole ages and dialects and Europes
away. The thought is enough
to wave away the generic sorrow of rain
and set fire to the umbrellas
of passing strangers and be soaked past bone's last cell.
A good thought, made of sadness
easily found in the body, residue
of one disaster or another—
sex collapsed like an old shed
and weariness pled
and tomorrow night maybe
and pulmonary half apologies caught in the mouth
of sleep. Her gone in time
or you gone, your eyes gone,
your feet on an endless carpet of old razors.
Something lost somewhere
inside you, untraceable, sinking,
and even at her heart's request
you'd never pluck a single shining coin
from behind her ear, the warm shell of all her sound,
in which you heard the ocean
rolling away in bracing violence.
In which more of you began to sink and be lost.
In which and in which
and this was enough
to put your lips to the door and not know why.
Not really. Not while rain
held its court in the world
and even in the noon darkness
the day gleamed with water on its face.

REMEMBER HOW SAD
THAT WAS WHEN

I missed sadness because I no longer missed you,
how emotionally counterintuitive it was
as my citizenship in the nation I made of you
gradually lapsed. I woke some other
place with lakes and blue skies and rush hours
and strangers I worried about. But no you.
No ages of you. No your name three times
when I walked somewhere or lay down at night
to bargain with sleep. No you
falling from my mouth everywhere I went.
No you anywhere to be seen.
A secret to keep. And mostly I did,
even beside other women who asked
with the privilege of their bodies
if you had ever existed and what did you do
and did you have a name I'd share
and had you been good to me
but I never gave you up. I left the last of you
to be lost in the fog inside me.
Napping in bomb craters, haggling
over debts I couldn't deny were mine,
memorizing every month's horoscope.
It seemed then the days
you had left me stained in sadness
were like that. Good apples on back order from God
and the steaks full of blood
you taught me to love, rationed.
At least I told myself this,
thinking of all the never you were.
But there were limits and lengths
and limits again. There were
songs inside the fog inside the world.

THINGS WE AGREED NOT TO SHOUT

Mom is dead. Dad melted. Again.
Bitter recriminations. Bitter infidelities. Bitter.
Streisand is on. Finnish curses on the firstborn
of everyone who held us back. My credit rating.
Your many catalogs of shame. Scrapbook time.

Do you remember where we sank the kindergarteners?

Infectious constipation. In our spare time,
we enjoy perfecting methods of evisceration.

Bingo. Also, fire. Let's make a baby.

Not anymore. You feel kind of weird inside.

My brother's indiscretions. My indiscretion
with your brother. That lost weekend in Vegas.
Landslide of therapy. Moving to another state. Again.

We are running out of America. Faster.
Right there. Good girl. Judas Priest lyrics.
Freebird. Woo. Random latitudes.

Imagined injuries. Getting tired of your meniscus.
Seriously. Routing numbers
and decade by decade
delineations of your bra sizes. Beginning with the seventies.

You promised. I thought you were
asleep. I thought you wouldn't mind it.

Surprise.

As you can already see, everything is fucked.
The shark wasn't working and Linda
had to be replaced by a homeless man
we cleaned up and taught crude
phonetic Russian. The Thai embassy threatened
dire things, canings and worse,
extraordinary rendition to French Canada,
if we refused to swear fealty
to their epileptic despot. He was deposed
in a coup while we were there
that everyone we met agreed
was fantastically bloody. I sent word
for the street urchins we'd chained
to a truck to be given cameras
and ankle bracelets that satellites can track
so we could find them
if they didn't return with the footage
I wanted. That's coming up
in just a second, though mostly all you see
is the road and a lot of running
and sobbing. The amount of viscera surprised
the crew, though to be fair,
I'd hired them off the back
of a loading dock in San Clemente
the week before. Scrappers, all of them,
and the severe language barriers
gradually thinned their numbers
as the shoot went on. Some we buried
within sight of a graveyard
out of respect for what we thought
their mother's stricken wishes might have been.
Some we tried to burn with
gasoline we siphoned from cars
or paint thinner we lifted from construction sites.
But it was all hypothetical
and in the heat we lost a few more
before we had a chance to pretend

our sadness was debilitating
or at least an emotion which passed for sadness
in that part of world. Look,
you can spot the shark again—
we made it out of packing foam
and spray-painted it ourselves
to make sure the job was done right.
We named it Bruce.
No one can say we didn't reasonably value *verité*.
And I do think it resembled
something a child or person recovering
from massive head trauma
would find dangerous or scary
or at least uncomfortable to be around.
We never did find Linda
though I left the number of the hotel
none of us were staying at
because we were sleeping in the jungle
taking turns at watch just like
this scene though the suspense is muted
by incorrect matting
so all you see is knees and fire
and some dialog about love
and honor and taking a stand
which was very moving to us all
though none of us wept
with our eyes on the trained chimp and his chainsaw.

MY INDEX OF SLIGHTLY
HORRIFYING KNOWLEDGE

Masturbation interrupted at Normandy
by strangers who fled sobbing to the surf.
Or by your mother, arrived early from Little Rock,
her muumuu throwing floral light at the wall.
Or by janitors at the Chinese Consulate.
By members of the Team Arthritis Tumbling Squad,
flush with the swagger of artificial hips.
By Richard Nixon, That Time He Came to Town
for Reasons Nobody Can Remember
but It's Commonly Agreed He Slept Over There.
By the priest and by that other priest
wearing a clever disguise. By Charles Nelson Reilly,
who seemed only vaguely offended
or disinclined to join in
or just bored, as one feels in the airport
of a connecting flight in a town everyone is leaving,
everyone knows it, and no one wants to be
the last one turning off all the lights,
one by one by one a part of the world turning to dust,
and, anyway, he died the other day
after long illness, which is another horror.
As is realizing encyclopedic fervor isn't a virtue.
Moving on.
Metaphysical constructs like Texas
and mayonnaise and cole slaw and vegan water parks
and The Bob Dylan Naked Network
and the strain of pernicious insanity
suffered by the curious. The id detonating
like an improvised explosive device.
The toxic spill of puberty.
That time. That time after that. The one before.
The encrypted slush of hotel pornography.
Snow covering the state. Facts about clouds.
Their immensity, the exact tonnage
of the crushing vapor sailing past like a camel.

Or a castle. That the hair and nails
of the dead only seem to grow
as the body recedes from itself like a flood.
The time she said no. The time she said yes.
The time she did not choose.
Her tired face in the morning. The mirror's interrogation.
The crafted answer. How you hate it.
Remedial rage. Nature all up in your grill.
The dolphin's prehensile penis,
fifteen inches in length and adroit
in the act of mating but not at dealing cards.
Or passing the salt or reaching
for the remote or that out of the way itch.
The monstrous seven feet
the blue whale lugs beneath the rolling waves
with disturbing extravagance
and the bifurcated penis of the marsupial
and the swan's feathered member
Zeus once took for his own
before falling like a cloud into Leda's lap.
The animals presumed by science to be extinct
only to be dragged dead into boats.
The brute coelacanth like a frayed epoch.
The Laotian rock rat coaxed from the caves of our guilt.
The ivory-billed woodpecker
flitting about the ancient ruins of Arkansas.
Bigfoot. Depending on who is asked
and whether his tenure status is certain.
Plesiosaurs. Because Polaroids of rotting flesh
weighing several hundred pounds
snagged by the crew of the *Zuiyo-maru*
off the coast of New Zealand in 1977
are really all you need to welcome them back to the party.
Weapons of mass destruction
or aluminum tubes or yellow cake

or the half-life of sweet, sweet Crisco
coursing the byways of my broken heart.
Decency and its granite headstone
for which Science designed
something based upon good taste and accurate data
and no funding. American
women who are able to belch
on command: 42 percent.
The Anti-Christ commanding them.
The rest of us trying to choose
between continued sentience
and celibacy so serious it borders on asexual fascism.
The stupor of powerlessness,
often confused with summer.
That guy with the shitbox van
with Valhalla crudely airbrushed on each side,
blissfully unaware
Ragnarok went down in the seventies.
Vain attempts at negotiating
with Kim Jong Il
who won't stop calling.
Kung fu masters who fill me
with existential dread
instead of broken bones.
But not the master of the ice-cream truck
who fills me with sugared variations on the theme of winter.
Memories of the woman I loved
for three pulverizing years
through the miseries of her marriage.
When she left me,
time's heartless crawl.
The librarian in the deathless stacks of orthodontic history.
My teeth aching like a beacon
in the darkness of my voice.
The butterfly threading its strange proboscis

through the flower's throat
for whatever it finds that to it is food.
A word like *dacrylphilia*,
which is to be aroused by the sight of tears.
The hook-handed man

who lifts my garbage with weird grace
and never a word to me.
The postman I nominate for a prosthetic conscience.
The man next door shooting cats
from the shade of his porch safari.
Who paints his house in Crimson Tide.
That town in which I once worked
and tried my best to live.
That town an August blister.
That town beside the black river.
That town and its roads tarred to muck.
Strangers who left the sweat of their hands on me
after asking or not asking
to petition the Lord and his angels
for my healing, Amen.
Strangers who stopped me in the street
or paid for my lunch
or wept over their dead son
or asked how many miles
in my wheelchair could I go.
The twenty-five miles in five hours
that would take me nowhere
except the car plant or pet food factory
the wind at night
would bring to everyone.
Crickets singing exact heat to the night.
Possums wild-eyed
and newborn pink all their mean lives.
Confederate flags limp in the windless past.
Abysmal roads leading everywhere.
The temptation of 1-800-CALL-JESUS signs.
The temptation of eighteen thousand Cracker Barrels.
The Ten Commandments like lunch menus everywhere.
The six and counting I'd ploughed through
with a kind of drunken force
though I never drank, leaving me memory like a septic sidekick.

Vestigial Ku Klux Klanism.
Vestigial seasons.
Defining vestigial.
Fried corn.

Governor Fob.
The child I babysat against my will
who would climb me like monkey bars
or claim he could use his penis as a bookmark.
That nightmare.
Pet store fish we bought
thinking it possible to release them in a spring pond
rife with thick reeds
and naïve exhilaration
for a few seconds only
until a wave, bluegill or pumpkinseed or what I don't know,
swallowed them.
That nightmare.
All of us meandering away from suicide.
Whistling past the graveyard. Stepping on the duck's humble
    grave.
Women who considered me
in their minds like an exotic equation.
The answer arrived at.
One kiss I could not follow down the steps she took.
And the virgin who loved me.
Whose love I reciprocated like politeness.
Whose meals I brought to her
where she was lost in work.
In accuracy. In data. In numbing repetition.
The microscopic souls she ferried
from dish to slide to blinding oblivion
and back again. The hours I watched
in drained solidarity. The elevator's escape.
The sky I wanted her to want
and not Sunday's corpse
and not Monday morning beside me,
ever untouched. Not Lazarus with the first light.
Not hurried into her clothes.
Or in them intransigent.
Not absent. Not in my arms like a fraction.
So it went.
But there were nights
when she would strip to nothing
in the bathroom's cheap fluorescence

and meekly meet me
in the fall of shower water
to soap the day from my skin
and in her hand make me come,
laughing as though this were magic new to a dying world.

OBLIVION:

LETTER HOME 1

Thanks for the bleach and the directions back,
even though we've had this discussion
already. I should tell you before I forget
or the crushing pain roars back
how much Emily appreciated the red yarn.
She couldn't stop smiling. Until
she vanished one night or decided
to leave. When I think how much the same
those are, even my bones sigh.
Down the street there are children
who need baths and when I find water,
I carry some in my hands and tell them
I've found another hidden river
in an owl's nest or inside one of the leaves
running mindlessly about
as the dead tend to do here.
I try to reveal their faces
or slick the knotted hair from their colorless eyes
or let them drink a little
but all they want to do is run.
I go back giving water to the ground
and names to their miner faces
and trying to recall the gloves I wore
when I was eleven. The trains I tried to believe
were only sound. The box
I sent you should be there before long,
though inside it all I placed
was a cricket's green leg.
I'm sorry about that but I was thinking of you.
It was all that I could afford
to send and it was all
I could find that was singing
that would not want to eat me
or wound me for sport

and before you ask, yes, I was careful,
though there were times
when all that saved my skin
were Grandma's prayers so give her my love.

OBLIVION:

LETTER HOME 2

Thanks for the cucumber lotion and coupons
you cut out of the Sunday paper
though I had to bury them in an old thermos
or sink them with bricks and twine
so nobody killed me. Reading the obituary
for Mr. Kondrackie was sad
though he once beat me with his cane
for guessing wrong. We all have our faults,
I think. Dad used to tell me that
before locking the door to the basement.
He'd spend weeks down there
with his electric putting range and German
films. Did you ever figure out
what he ate? I think about that
when the glow of major cities burning
is strangely beautiful. Almost comforting.
I've been fixing up an old culvert
cannibals once used for a stop-over latrine.
It takes a lot of imagination
but I think you'd be proud
of the flow from one end to the other.
It's been raining here all week.
And according to the woman
who pitied me during the night
and wanted nothing for her time
or the shadow of her body near the fire,
three years have gone by,
all of them marked by endless rain.
It seems hard to believe.
The people here are nice.

The ones capable of more than
savagery or tandem autoerotic asphyxiation,
at least. The food is bad
and you wouldn't care for it
in that it barely exists.

But it's been good for me.
When I laid the rags I wore
beside the woman
who had been cold when I found her,
I wasn't afraid.
I never once thought of you.
Write back soon. Tell everyone I'm not dead.

OBLIVION:
LETTER HOME 3

Thanks for the rubber glue and instruction book
with VHS video and stereo cassette about
reenacting famous battles in American history,
including Korea and Bhutan. Before
his death in Thailand, Dad had good things
to say about the plasticity of time
in the modern age. I never understood
why he would take the reel-to-reel recorder
I earned from selling *Grit* for sixteen dark years.
Why he put it in the freezer before
retreating to the backyard where men could burn
things with epithelial disregard.
Which reminds me. A burning thing pursued me
this morning for several miles.
You'd think there'd be a lot of noise.
Screaming. Wailing. Existential checks bouncing
like basketballs all over the place.
Me seriously losing my shit.
But it was quiet. My frayed breath
and the fire's placid respiration
like the soundtrack to something minimalist.
Lars von Trier, if he took the burning stick from his ass.
I wanted to tell you about it
before I forgot. At night distant walls crumble.
You feel a thump through the earth.
I haven't learned to ignore it
so I wake inside something horrid.
Industrial throat after industrial throat.
Once in the ruins of an outhouse.
Or what I thought was one,

though by now everything unburned is amazingly fouled.
And by this I mean
this is one gift even you
would confess is their mastery,
with your white gloves, ultraviolet lights

and night-vision goggles
watching me shed my virginity.
I think about her a lot—
I can't remember the color of her eyes.
A song was playing
on the radio by the window.

POISON

I never thought I'd tire of being a mammal:
the flexible hair, the summers off,
the endless sweetness of milk,
the half ecstasy of live birth
duking it out with the napalm fever
so much death engenders. But fire ruined
me, at least it ruined my teeth:
what once were grim experts
at ripping raw beast from the bone
turned soft when food did
over fire. Served mush, mammalian teeth
slipped away, smaller each
millennium. Ours are the worst
in all the animal kingdom
and when I look to the marmot's face,
to the mongoose's maw
meant for the cobra's white flesh,
I see my better. No matter
how deep into darkness I diagram the trebuchet,
or feather the arrow's fletch,
the stone pried from the river
is still the river's tooth
and the throb of blood in my hammered thumb
I suck like a poison
I want.

REGARDING YOUR APPLICATIONS
FOR MANY IMAGINARY POSITIONS

Regarding your applications for many imaginary positions,
such as Glorious Leader of the Lutheran Jihad,
which you were good enough to explain
would pay no salary and convey no health benefits
or even obligate us to acknowledge you
as a fellow human being, we wish to thank you
for every assurance your tendency
toward unfettered rage is in your past,
and that a movie like *A Clockwork Orange*
or the good parts of *Saving Private Ryan*
would give us an idea of how you'd wasted
the best years of your life. All of us
nodded when we saw ourselves in you
and your poignant cries for help
even as we forwarded them to the legal department.
We trust you don't mind.
We appreciate your seemingly robotic sense
of initiative and attention to detail,
to say nothing of the shockingly candid
photographs of you in bed with your girlfriend,
though we respectfully suggest
there are very few women who enjoy
what the professionally shot set
appears to show you doing,
and further we have reason to believe
you picked her up on Ninth Street
behind the weird carwash
one night when the desperation was too much to bear.
That is why it gives us no pleasure
to say we have found someone else
who best seems to fit our imaginary needs
at this time. Not only do we wish you luck,
we wish you would stop burning effigies across the street.

. . . and I will be your Lighthouse of Alexandria, waiting to
be dismantled, wanting it. I will wait in my cubicle, I will keep the
coffee going, keep it hot. No, boiling. No, scalding. I'll research the
flashpoint of coffee. I will come back from Colombia burdened
with fragrant beans. Call me Juan. Where is my burro? Milk,
sugar, cream. Anything. Tell me. I'm begging you. My favorite
word is *servile*. It's not my middle name but it can be. I have the
paperwork. Already filled out. Already signed. I had my spleen
removed, one kidney, the appendix poisonous with mystery, all
to make room for my experimental onboard fax machine, just for
this moment. Just for you. No eye contact, yes, I remember. Every
morning I practice not looking at myself. I pretend I'm you. I
pretend I'm a storm cloud. I just pretend. It passes the time when
I'm not here. When I'm not working. When my sebaceous glands
don't hum their worksong. You should hear it. But no one can.
Not even me. In my dreams I'm chased by you. But you're made
of bees. You're that man with a beard of bees. You're my boss. Yes.
I love my cubicle. I want to keep it. Some days I think I'd kill for
it. I think you could understand that. Maybe. Just maybe. I think
there is a kind of darkness in our hive. It reminds me of stars.
But not stars, not exactly. I think my intention is to speak of the
universe, to say something, to not be this. I'm filling up paper
with my signature, if only to perfect it. To recognize some part of
myself. To not wake up ever again in that sick light of the train
station, with no idea how I got there. Thinking only that the '70s
had been detonated there. Thinking only I'd never escape. That
it would always be winter. Never not Philadelphia. Bleak forever
and ever, amen. That's my prayer, even though I'm violently
agnostic, allergic to order. Except here. Except here. My own
personal Jesus. He was just here. You didn't see? Next time I'll find
you. I'll come running. I'll stop what I'm doing. Unless it's work.
Unless I'm working. I'll work it out. I'll train small rodents. I'll
burn something. Myself if I have to. Like that awful picture of the
monk, dead on his knees, all of him flame. Self-immolation is the
term, I believe. This call to fire is holy. Sometimes I think you're
holy, you're fire, and I laugh and begin to break things. I throw
potted ferns from the roof. Once, a tricycle. I watched it descend

and I said my name, my whole name, just before it busted cheaply far below. And then, then, I am so sad, so heartbroken, so perfect and abject, all that's left is to wait for the moon to slowly flash in the sky like a bulb. I don't pay much attention to the stars, so many of them dead, expired, exploded, but still showing up in the sky, grief so long delayed it isn't grief. It's just light and unlight. And there are hours left before work again and I am in my suit already and my tie isn't silk, it's rope like you said.

MY NIGHTMARE

My nightmare isn't falling or even falling
naked with strangers amused
by what I try each day to hide,
this biology of strangeness,
no, my nightmare isn't forgetting
my pants because that sounds
suspiciously like fun
or at least some sort of joyful malfeasance
orchestrated in rain
while dogs bark manic interrogations
in the night and buckshot
rings through the dark
and I'm singing your name
to some randomly selected forgotten god.
To be distracted by pleasure
isn't my nightmare
but it once was before
all the cartilage inside
hardened to bone
and I marveled at the ear
you never allowed anyone to kiss, not even me,
and maybe that was
a kind of nightmare,
that refusal. No one ever warned me
to fear my hands
but they should have
known the things they would do
or not do. The knobs turned and knots undone
because there is
pleasure in erasure.
Once you let me watch you
bathe, the tub sudded with lilac froth.

We hardly spoke as the water cooled.
The soap fell from your skin.
You were new.
Beside you I failed to dream of anything else.

BAD MOOD

Bad mood and bad dog and bad luck like
my broken neck or heart or head
playing out so much bad weather
like kinked yarn unraveled by a bad
black cat, which summons luck again,
that diffident lover half
naked in the dark. To her
I walked beneath one thousand ladders
over miles of bad road
ribboned with bad directions.
Which wasn't as bad
as I thought it would be.
My bad ear pressed to the powdery wall
behind which strangers
badly performed their bad sex,
their bored flesh
nothing like the paleness of tulips
in the heat of Alabama
or the severed second
in which our voices sunk
from the bad phones we carried with us.
Across that bad connection,
the bad things compelling us
to speak out, to end up, to say
even now my skin flecks away.
Like paint applied
badly, quickly to cover
some previous horror,
some bad end solved badly,
the evidence lost,
thrown out, awarded to the jury of dust.
But I said it wasn't so bad.
And it wasn't.
There were days when knives of noon light
sliced the sky apart like tangerines.
And there were hours
and words amounting to consolation

and entire towns
ripe with welcome,
surrendering their thousand mirrors,
their seven long years.

ACCENT

Werner Herzog, I'm trying to speak like you,
though outside autumn wildly arcs
and the Alps are only a word I have
loved a long time. Tired is not
what I want my body to be
but a mist above snow. So I'm pretending
this Teutonicism. Jackhammers
through lake ice. Rabid flocks
of woodpeckers immune
to migraine but not so much hunger.
Last week I learned this,
that recycled glass has a name.
That it's *cullet*. I thought of Faulkner,
his mongrel personae. Which
is to say I thought of
suffering and fire and the south,
to which I am speaking
like a fool. Amused in my flesh,
even by my flesh, though
lovers never laughed. Sighed appropriately,
called out, murmurations
and writhing. In my mouth
I held them as well. All of you,
come back, my nerves seem
to clearly say, though mumbling
I've said the direst things
or stopped one at my door
in muslin dreams, her body specked
with paint. *Longer still*
won't you stay is what I meant though
what I said I cannot say.

MY ARMS

My arms are mostly cosmetic. When I say this
to a stranger, often he'll wince
like he wants to hide inside his eyes.
Vanish from the day. I shouldn't laugh,
should be tired twenty-one years
into the telling of a poor joke,
made of pain, nerves snuffed like wicks. Back
then, I was a boy. No secret
that I fell through that
summer like a star. And here I am
wanting spring and birdsong
after tedious winter. Once I prayed
my arms might serve me
again, roll toothpaste from the tube,
dump rice into boiling water,
swat dead the mosquito
drilling its derrick face
through my skin. That symmetry,
left and right, one and one—
it's not a math I know,
not anymore. There are days I want
to lament broken glass
or put my fist through the door
or throttle the blue sky's silent
throat. There are nights
full of ache, full of nothing nimble.
No music but smashed guitars
would be enough. How many clasps
and how many buttons
did I try with my teeth
until her hands did for me what I could not?
Untrue to say I lost count
of what I never hoped to keep.
A lie to say that when
she held my hands to her hips
and her body above mine,
I loved such need, I did not hate us both.

PREEMPTIVE ELEGY

Another future I don't want to believe in:
my body filled with me slabbed in ice,
victim of comic book conflagration
involving great powers and absurd scheming
and slights darkly nursed over the years
and monologues refined and refined
for the day that had to come when Fate
evened things out, made right or bearable
the wrong and unbearable, brought low
the high and mighty, raised up the low and once weak—
and me stumbling in on it all,
looking for the bathroom or the gift shop,
blasted northward to the Pole.
Assumed dead and left to dream endless cold.
And there would be the scientists
to find me and thaw me
back at Ice Station Zebra with hair dryers
because they were bored
or out of large caliber ammunition
or had forgotten where the helicopter was parked
or were just crazed by isolation.
Stunned when my body spasmed in the air.
When all the lights began again
to flicker inside the defrosted wad of brain.
When the shock had passed
and we devised elaborate hand signals
because they spoke languages
that sounded a lot like other languages
but not my own. A day or two
and black floods of coffee
would determine the years
and the worlds I had slept away.
And the you. Who mourned me
however long, however brokenly you needed.
And all the rest of your life
dodging the rage of others
and keeping sparse gardens

and a lot of pragmatic, hurried showers.
Which is reason enough
to be sad. To mourn
your tangled hair with my thawed heart.

AIRPORT LETTER 2

I left my heart in Phuket, I sang, lifting
from the emerald earth, table tray
stowed before me in obedience
to her voice. Or her boredom, paining
me. That we should have
all this sun but want sleep
and more sleep or a vat of bruised gin
was unbearable. With me
I had no books and no paper
on which to diagram sentences
in Esperanto. I read the air sickness bag
inviting me to advertise
on its side my product
and had to smile. Remind me never
to resist. Remind me
to produce something this year
but not a child,
nothing that will have my eyes
or begin to speak this foreign language.
I thought of you beneath
the zaftig clouds. The sun dropping
though them like a lustrous
bomb. The ganglion of roads running
out into the night. Looking
for small birds is instructive
but only in rage
and infinite humility. I'm learning
geography is about loss
and so I keep moving
into closets that never smell like you.
I'm learning not to order
everything and want nothing.
My mouth is empty. The words won't stay.

. . . and I will help you lose my two hundred pound wheelchair somewhere in Toronto. I will laugh like a marrow-fat hyena when you call it my chariot. When you mention Stephen Hawking. Or Christopher Reeve. Because you are the first, the only, the original, the initiator, the big dog, the supreme wit. I will nod serenely. I will identify with your sister in a wheelchair. Or your cousin. Or your pet whimpering at home. Yes, lupus is sad. I will never not be sad. Just for you. I'll be happy when you say. When you dispense Jesus to me like candy, I will shout amen. I will let Him melt in my mouth but not in my hand. I am shouting amen right now. I am melting. If you can't hear me, then deafness too is sad. Let's be sad awhile.

I don't need my knees—bash away. The bruises can't last long enough to suit me. Yes, that hurts but it's ok. When you drop me in the aisle, I won't complain. I'll apologize for not falling faster. I'll get to work on speeding up terminal velocity. Stephen Hawking will help me. We are brothers. He will text me something brilliant tonight. We talk about the stars. We talk about the new bodies Reeve promised. It's the NHL for me. I will punch Gretzky in his Canadian face. In Toronto. I will lose somebody else's chair in that white, white city. Traditions must be observed.

I will ride the bus all day with a veteran from the USS *Bob Hope*. I will take the drinking straws from his hair and frame his crumpled xeroxes of Bill Clinton and this will all be intensely normal. I will marry the non plus ultra sized woman screaming Jesus' sweet name to me. I will move fifteen feet over because that wasn't a bus stop. This is. I'll build my little pink house right there. My Amish jelly will never again be confiscated. The Amish will scare us no more.

I'll interrupt oral sex beside the Delaware River because there's no ramp down to my hotel. The shadow of one more bridge will fold me up, will hide me from the world. Just for a while. A sad while. There are no other whiles. I will agree instantly. I will agree great strides have been made. I will stride. I will smile but I'll be thinking of your lupus. Your sister's lupus. Is she pretty? I hope so. I will text her Neruda but claim it's my own. I will seem at last like a genius. Call me Stephen.

And I will love your tasteless waffles and not loudly announce your free coffee tastes like ass. I won't do that. Not again. I made promises. I'll wait patiently like a Hummel figurine. I will cherish my skin of dust while you send my luggage to Cincinnati and me to hell. Which is the Airport Marriot. I will covet the complimentary toiletries. I will cover my broken body in your free Colgate. I will be white, white, white. Except for the bruises. And I will miss my chariot and I will be sad and try to tell myself I'm not coming down with lupus and Gerald Ford won't ever stop being dead.

SEMI-APOCALYPTIC R.S.V.P.
WITH CONTINGENCIES

Barring the return of plague-like oral rot,
as predicted by many licensed dental technicians
and one judicious massage therapist,
who visibly shook near the spot
where her lime Camry had been,
coupled with your ability to construct
on-site Level-5 biohazard containment facilities
able to incinerate frozen solids;

despite the roving bands of College Republicans
responsibly marauding through America
with their bloodless fables of fiscal insanity
and sexual defenestration
and genetic opportunity for all;

despite the spontaneous emotional evisceration
inflicted by red-haired Michiganders
accustomed to spearing fish through the ice;

despite the chronic shame of Provo,
against which I am powerless
like all men who live in this age
sporting seething erections while talk radio dissembles;

and assuming the rivers that day
don't run with the blood
of innocent linebackers and their enablers;

assuming the paralytic joy of childhood never returns;

despite the many things I stole
just to feel something, anything;

as long as they are linked
to the blind-mute in whose house I left them

after typing up confessions
to many crimes and insecurities;

despite stubbing my soul every night
for the past seven hundred years;

and unless there is nothing better on television,
and there never is,
like *How to Attract the Government's Most Solemn Attention,*
which seemed like a bad idea to me
but was fascinating all the same;

and in case the Latvian succubus does not survive,
even after the truly surreal cost
and the difficulty of housing her
in a system of underground bunkers,
which are still tastefully furnished
because I'm not an animal;

and unless I haven't fully recovered
from the sprained knee
suffered last week in a pick-up game with the guys;

assuming witnesses dredged
from the quarry's alkaline depths
don't recover well enough to recall
their bad luck that night in May
when I was bowling with my lupus-stricken mother
after recording the progression
of her grotesque deformities,
an activity which pleased her
for as long as Science still considered her human;

and assuming the resolution of many long-standing debts
to dark personages and princes of power

who would enjoy the sport of my body
dragged through most of Laredo
until they were bored or nothing was left but a sleeve,

then I would be very glad to attend
the white wedding of your ass-faced daughter.

SEDUCTION WITH MONOMYTH

No, you never asked for this
cyclopean storm of single entendre valentines,
never filled out an online form
or faux-casually mentioned
to your Nereid neighbor
the slot machine odds of your deepest
desire. No, you never
requested assistance of the half-
literate pool boy Pablo
with his arms whisking leaves from the dead-
end mirror of the water
and waited for him
in the shadow of lust,
in frail frill. In a cloud,
you thought, in a cloud
and in a cloud, forever and ever,
Amen. No. Men
who are paid to think
in obscurity, whom I envy
without quite knowing it,
say clouds might feel
spongy, almost walkable, a crème
of slow descent. You
never thought of me
in my obscurity
beneath these theoretical clouds
which say rain. Which say
you can never escape
a single thing. But
here I am, with flowers, poems,
darling failures aplenty,
daring your sense
of misguided charm
to kick in, the thousand strange
verbs rustling
in my mouth
like scabby autumn. No,

I never asked
for this weather,
this brine-happy sky,
but in it I go. This nervy instant. This.

BORDERING ON THE TRAGIC

We kept hearing good things about Muncie.
There were meat-eating flowers
in the very same world. Ravenous weeds.
A long time I watched her kiss
the waitress she held like a secret.
I watched her drop like a tooth into ink.
She never told me.
When I left, children sang.
When they sang, the world was less a riddle.
All the dreams were deciduous.
Litter in the night. Scant cities
dumping light in the sky.
Who could say to them the sky had enough?
The birds rattled bones
time had hollowed for flight.
The children had tried to sing like them,
their belongings in bandanas
knotted to switches swung
across their baby-fat shoulders.
I was never proud to pitch bricks
through bakery windows
when it was dark, to sift glass for crumbs.
That was hunger, I think,
though I never feared
the end of my body
beneath the trees where I hid from time.
Ambulances sang
about blood, blood forever.
Through green wood I heard every hymn.
And then they'd pass into the silence of others.
Whose hearts splintered.
And I hadn't caused it,
not in my distance
or in all the nearness I had left,
but to the air I confessed all the same.

ELEGY FOR THE PLESIOSAUR
ON THE ADVENT OF ITS
PREDICTED RETURN

We find your bones all the time and try not to be sad.
We're not even sure how late we were
to your funeral or whether we sent flowers
or told great stories of how you lived
on your own terms and without regret
and that for you the most important thing
was family. And awesome displays of predation.
Carbon dating can't say whether
the toasts we raised to you and your epoch
would have burned your alien face
with embarrassment for all the wildness of your youth
or swallowed you up in laughter,
as you might have tried to swallow us
on another day in the long life of ancient hunger.
And we hope the words we said
to all the mates you'd won with rituals
impossible for mammals to even comprehend
helped to assuage the thing that was grief
that was in them and would never fade,
they swore by the dangerous volume of their tears
and the veils of black weed
they wore in the fathoms of bereavement.
To your children looking on you
who said to themselves that you only slept
and would wake when all this was over
and everyone had left who swore
to honor your last hunt with all theirs to come,
we can only theorize how much they felt
of our terrified stabs at consolation
and whether they would have
let us keep our arms. The fossil record
so far contains no evidence
we attended the deposition of your body

as it was lowered into the murk
while many beasts sadly lowed in the depths
or whether the tears finally came
when upwards we desperately kicked
to the air of the world that was soon to be our own.

PRAISE

Your whole life might pass without thinking
of the debt of gratitude you owe
Walt Disney. Thank you, Walt, for Goofy,
the man-dog hybrid, wherever you are
cryogenically contained, cheating death
in that bunker beneath one ride
or the other. Thinking of this, I'm invaded
by happiness. I can't even sigh
as the autumn sky deepens like your breath,
anonymous former lover, to whom
these poems are always piping
up, in what no one has ever called the axilla
of the night. Meaning, I think
of you when it's unbearably dark
and the world has drawn so close
my face no longer dreams of secret proximities.
Just dull air. Thank you, lungs,
for abiding even still, for never leaving
your obscure posts within the pink
shell of my aerobic life, my life humming
with heat. And thank you, Godard,
for saying the only things
a good movie needs are a girl and a gun.
In agreement I admit I am
tingling. In the silvered light,
I'm dreaming of the red-haired girl
and the murderous gun, like a bazooka.
Thank you, Elegantly Branded Suburban Utility Vehicle,
for not running me down each day
I stop to speak to fenced-in schnauzers
who hate me for my freedom.
Thank you, blessed
velocity. Thank you, blessed
thirst for oil. I'm thirsty, too,
though this would surprise
no one I loved, who helped define
for me the idea of direct address,

and it's your hair fanning out in the waters
of each sad poem and your heart
that was amazingly cruel
and thank you, living world,
that you don't cease, that you go on and on and on.

AT NIGHT, IN NOVEMBER, TRYING NOT
TO THINK OF ASPHODEL

I'm no use for parties, for the idle language
which is all how hellish are the days
and dark or where did I find
that thread count or what do I think must be
done about et cetera. So I smile
and nod and never say much,
happy to be thought impaired
or mute and when asked
to name what I couldn't live without
were I marooned on a desert island,
I say viable organs. Not a book and its pages
slipping from cheap binding
and not an album
that's not an album
but summer's totem forever
and not one deft lover
and not the red ringlets
of her hair let down in a grotto beside the sea.
To be consigned there,
to that island, that home
to the fetish of consolation,
is nothing I ever want
to want. To be stripped of desire
as if it were a bandage.
But here in the night made of alarms,
a train shambles
through the dark
and it's hard to hear the trees speaking
the language we made
for them. Or I did,
thinking of you
who taught me regret.
There are nights when I dream
of stolen oranges.
How we ran away with the sun in our arms.

And there are nights
when I can't speak,
not even to the wind
in the strange tongue of the dark pine trees.

BEGINNING IN THE LOST AND UNCLAIMED BAGGAGE CENTER IN SCOTTSBORO, ALABAMA

In that tumble of flotsam, that hall
of the mishandled and shunted
and slightly damaged and mostly never missed
except maybe to curse
the constant loss living is,
I couldn't be consoled, though I snickered
the same as we all did
rifling the racks of red negligees,
faux satin and wrongly furred
and crotchless and sexlessly peek-a-boo
there in the open air
far from the foreign nights
for which each had been
bought in arterial glee or shame
and one of them I tried to imagine
in an Eden not wholly defiled
but I couldn't be consoled,
not even by the strangeness of the sacred
undergarments worn by Mormons
beneath their clothes when inside the temple,
that one of us bought
to wear for Halloween,
the long coveralls stitched with arcanum
meant to keep
the wearer from all harm,
meant to be secret
like all the wretched lace lost before love or after it
but fated for Alabama
and the mockery
that was our boredom,
a kind of karmic piling on
that hardly seemed right or fair
but there it was,

and there we all were
in the night bleeding heat
while in the magnolia's branches
dying locusts sang to us only scorn.

AUSTRIA

Easy in a college town to hang Klimt
from your many times repaired wall
or life and easy to think this better,
somehow, than violence or routine
or the kaleidoscopic degradations each waitress
in her kindness prepares
for you. Lord, a long time
I have thought of what more there is
to say. Lord, I have thought
this. Sometimes committed my flesh
to unbearable action
if only to gain speed in retreat.
If only to wake in the dark strangeness
of agreements: falsehoods
and broken words and spasms
of summer. And now a loveliness passes
and it does not matter
of what it is made or when
or living and named and nightly possessed.
Lord, it does not matter
that any of us keep on
but we do. In great numbers,
in harrowing efficiencies,
we cannot do anything but this
persistence that will not go.
I am trying, Lord, to love this world,
however it is fated
to end. Behind the wall a girl
is making love.
Two rooms distant I can hear her
and want to leave
even through the spill of rain.
But I stay because
there is nothing to leave
my mind will not carry with it
in a kind of tortured attentiveness.
I know her name

if only by her business card
given to me like I would have a use for it.
Like I had waited there
for her name. Not
all my life but a devoted time.
What else but her name and her nerves unspooling now
could I wait for? Besides
silence. Or mercy.
Or deafening rain. Her sign to now, now,
Lord, be still.

ELEGY FOR THE LUMBERING MONSTER

Vaya con Cthulhu is what I always say
in moments like these though
it tends towards wasted sentiment
in the best, most literary ways,
and, anyway, I'm struck by your end,
your unremarked end, your ragged
fin de siècle demise, and I wonder
if you have even been informed
that all your shambling power is gone—
that nobody thinks of you anymore,
abject blips of terror pinging
about in the catacombs of the heart.
From your cheaply adorned sarcophagus,
a word which means flesh
eating, you stumbled out
as though you were in no hurry
except to make your listless, plaintive hymn.
And this was supposed to be
an eternal horror, but to us
now you're plucky more than evil,
determined in a way that
Americans can never get enough of,
zombified in the brine
of our own apocalyptic zeal.
I wonder if you know,
if you understand your fallen place,
now that all our beasts,
our lithe undead, our sprinting succubae,
have broken away, aerobic,
clawing at the subcompact
in wild reverse, the steering wheel slick
with undetermined blood,
the tires smoking sickly on the black
ribbon of asphalt,
which I cannot help but remind
is made of other dead
beasts: the allosaur, the brachiosaur,

the suddenly wiped-out
for reasons we don't know
and so are fascinated,
imagining the black horizon's end.
My own end is what
we don't speak of,
though in the marbled blindness of your eyes
it's easy to imagine.
And I do but away from me I run.

A LONG TIME I'VE WANTED
TO SAY SOMETHING

A long time I've wanted to say something
and not know the next word until
it busied my mouth. Love talk, anger, consolation,
lies, mad hints at the edge of green
water where fish and snakes swam
weirdly away from my lonesome post—
five dozen kinds of greetings
and one of severance
entered this conversation
I am having with the earth.
O world, I want to love you
better than I do, forgiving
every satellite dish bolted to the roof
and pointed towards the
ubiquity of the sky,
and all it holds within it like a gravid cloud—
darkness first of all
and then the post-mortem flare of the stars,
and fixed between both,
satellites soaking our cells
with beamed, invisible pornography
and all its stark frustrations,
its spacey coupling, its theater of vicious hunger.
How many times have I gone
home through that rain,
my body perforated by
waves of strange ecstasy?
World, I've wanted to box you
on your huge ear, or hide
something from you
that you badly want, right then, that instant,
this now. I've wanted
to pour you out
until you're empty,

worth filling up again.
I am not talking to you,
anymore. Tired
as I am of gravity
and tired as I am
of my bones, the sullen sameness of their pain,
let me just whistle
a sad song
into the newness of the air.
Let me plan out,
let me devise and arrange
and braid one lost
path to the next.
Let me save something from vague peril.
It is all around us,
after all, danger,
or love, or war,
or spontaneous jamborees on a hilltop littered with fiddles.
I am thinking of love.
Which means in my tongue
that I am praying for it
to be saved from never knowing me.

MY LUCK

for Eliot K. Wilson

That day I spilled milk with crossed fingers
didn't make sense but the tears did
even though the laws of science insist
there's no sense in mourning
waste. At least, I think it's science
but it could be philosophy—
in school I hated all of that.
I tried to think of a world
in which wisdom was optional
but that world had thought of me first.
My best friend toils in a land
named Minnesota where sunlight is also optional.
A long time ago
everyone attempted not to weep
or blaspheme or run screaming
into the scarred arms of the past
waiting in official gloom like an abusive lover
and though I wasn't there
the day was relentlessly pleasant
and not many died
unless it was an option
they'd been considering for a long time
and what I mean to say
is that I'm capable of Truth.
You might doubt the veracity of all this.
So many times I've lied
my way into your beds and back out again,
it isn't funny. Except it's hilarious
and painful and exhausting and cathartic and untrue.
All at once,
a metaphysical hernia.
I'm not sure why I'm here
or how the air can seem to scald everyone,
everyone in plain sight,

so I wait out the day's thin patience
playing games of chance
I'm not certain I fully grasp
or even enjoy distracted as I am
by the mutter of rust,
the mewl of rescued kittens,
the sky broken by blunt star light.

MY MOCK-SCALE DREAM

In my neoprene monster skin, in my faux city
stormy with hellfire, in my broken
down dollhouse, in my tiny bed
that sleeps my toe, in my souvenir
sombrero, in that noontime shade
badly needed, in my die-cast
Corvette, cherry red, sun bright, comet
fast, in that shrunken hour
I cannot hold on to, in that dwindled dawn,
beneath that ancient sapling,
beneath that cobbled sky,
beneath those wheeling stars,
addled by light, always light, let me go,
allow me the democratic darkness
and my pillow over my morning face,
give me that, give me your face,
whoever you are, forever perfected stranger,
your skin, and my skin,
my monstrous skin,
my time by the river
tiresomely returned to
and the slurred water going by
no music at all,
before all things immense,
before that water
like night, in which I dropped
my watch or was it
a stone warm from my hand
or the sun's adumbrations
or nothing at all,
that hunger you tried to cure,
I am saying directly this painful, pained thing,
I am saying it will not last,
my fist for my mouth
plugging up
this hole, this endless, this always, this never.

ACKNOWLEDGMENTS

My thanks to Richard Jackson, Rodney Jones, Lucia Perillo, and Edward Brunner—teachers and friends alike.

Further thanks go to Victoria Chang, Wendy Wisner, Aimee Nezhukumatathil, Suzanne Frischkorn, Bob Hicok, Bruce Smith, Joel Brouwer, C. Dale Young, Keith Montesano, Ander Monson, Melanie Jordan, Alex Lemon, David Hernandez, Cynthia Roth, Matt Guenette, Ruth Daugherty, Adrian Matejka, Stacey Brown, Bradley Paul, Karri Paul, Laurel Snyder, Taylor Loy, Rebecca Shelton, Mark Womack, Stephanie Walker, and June Yang.

And love to my friends, colleagues, and family in Carrollton: Chad Davidson, Greg Fraser, Gwen Davidson, Jane Hill, Bob Hill, Jonette Larrew, Jade Kierbow, and Adam Turner.

Special thanks to the Whiting Foundation and to the Department of English and Philosophy at the University of West Georgia for their invaluable support.

And, last, to Betsy Lerner, all my gratitude.

"My Life Among," "Airport Letter 1," and "My Mock-Scale Dream" appeared in *The Southern Review*.

"Rented Dark," "To-Do List," "Elegiac Forecast," "Accent," "Preemptive Elegy," "Elegy for the Plesiosaur on the Advent of Its Predicted Return," and "Beginning in the Lost and Unclaimed Baggage Center in Scottsboro, Alabama" appeared in *New Orleans Review*.

"Airport Letter 2" appeared in *Ecotone*.

"Early in a New Year" and "Praise" appeared in *Keep Going*.

"A Brief History of History" appeared in *Black Warrior Review*.

"My Past" appeared in *Willow Springs*.

"The Lives of the Optimists" and "One More Theory about Happiness" appeared in *Pebble Lake Review*.

"Valentine" appeared in *Burnside Review*.

"Loyalty Oath" and "Remember How Sad That Was When" appeared in *River Styx*.

"My Index of Slightly Horrifying Knowledge" appeared in *The Missouri Review*.

"Oblivion: Letter Home 1," "Oblivion: Letter Home 2," "Bordering on the Tragic," "At Night, in November, Trying Not to Think of Asphodel," and "Austria" appeared in *Diode*.

"Poison" appeared in *32 Poems*.

"My Nightmare" appeared in *Redivider*.

"My Arms" appeared in *Crazyhorse*.

"Eulogy" and "Bad Mood" appeared in *42 Opus*.

"User's Guide to Physical Debilitation" appeared in *The Paris Review*.

"A Long Time I've Wanted to Say Something" appeared in *The Kenyon Review*.

© STARR THOMISON

ABOUT THE AUTHOR

PAUL GUEST's first book, *The Resurrection of the Body and the Ruin of the World,* won the 2002 New Issues Prize in Poetry, and his second book, *Notes for My Body Double,* won the 2006 Prairie Schooner Book Prize. His latest book is a memoir, *One More Theory About Happiness.* The recipient of a 2007 Whiting Writers' Award, he lives in Atlanta, Georgia.